TO Lennon

HAPPY BIRTHDAY

FROM Grandmother March.

HAPPY BIRTHDAY

..................., which piñata has the candy inside?

Shake the book really fast....

Come on, ...,
let's **POP** the balloons.

Ready?... Set?...
Go!

Press here
....

READY? SET? SMILE ...

Time for a funny
birthday selfie,

....

IT'S MY
BIRTHDAY

HA, HA,

it's upside down! Turn the book

..............................,

to see who's monkeying around.

Ready for your
big present,
.....................?

Tilt the book
this way....

HAPPY
BIRTHDAY

Happy Birthday

....

Now take a big
breath in and
BLOW
out your candles.

3, 2, 1...

MY FAVORITE PARTY GAME IS:

HAPPY BIRTHDAY

MY AMAZING PARTY GUESTS ARE:

Draw your cake

HAPPY BIRTHDAY

Illustrated by Hazel Quintanilla
Designed by Nicky Scott

Copyright © Orangutan Books Ltd 2020

Sourcebooks and the colophon are registered trademarks of Sourcebooks, Inc.
All rights reserved.

Published by Sourcebooks Wonderland,
an imprint of Sourcebooks Kids
P.O. Box 4410, Naperville, Illinois 60567-4410
(630) 961-3900
sourcebookskids.com

Date of Production: January 2020
Run Number: 5017044
Printed and bound in China (GD)
10 9 8 7 6 5 4 3 2 1